This SpongeBob SquarePants Holiday Annual belongs to

....

nickelodeon

SPONGEBOB SQUAREPANTS

Holiday Annual

EGMONT
We bring stories to life.

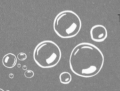

First published in Great Britain 2011
by Egmont UK Limited
239 Kensington High Street, London W8 6SA

**Watch every day
on Nickelodeon!
www.nick.co.uk**

Text by Pippa Shaw. Designed by Catherine Ellis.

ISBN 978 1 4052 5645 2
1 3 5 7 9 10 8 6 4 2
Printed in China

Contents

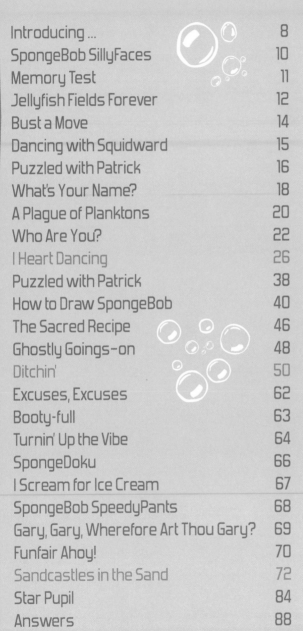

Introducing ...

SpongeBob SquarePants

Star **Fry-Cook** at the
Krusty Krab and all round
good Sponge.

Patrick Star

SpongeBob's best friend
who **lives under a
rock**. Likes being
SpongeBob's best friend
and living under a rock.

miaow!

Gary

SpongeBob's pet snail.
Can tie his own
shoelaces.

Squidward Tentacles

SpongeBob's neighbour and colleague at the Krusty Krab. Thinks he is the smartest guy in the whole of Bikini Bottom (and SpongeBob is the stupidest).

Mr Krabs

Owner of the Krusty Krab and biggest money-lover in the whole of Bikini Bottom.

Plankton

Tiny microbe owner of the Chum Bucket, college graduate and Mr Krabs' nemesis. Has a computer wife called Karen. His ultimate dream is to take over the world.

Sandy Cheeks

Originally from Texas but now lives in her treedome under the sea. Likes karate. Hi-yaaa!

SpongeBob SillyFaces

One advantage of having a **sponge** for a body is that SpongeBob can pull **great faces**, as well as being great at soaking up spilt liquids.

Get out **a mirror** or, better still, sit facing a friend and try pulling all the **same faces as SpongeBob**. Put a tick next to the one that made you **laugh** the most.

TRUE OR FALSE?
SpongeBob is made of coral.

Memory Test

It's fair to say that **Patrick's memory** isn't his strongest point.

See if **your memory** is any better with this memory test. Look at this picture of SpongeBob and Patrick visiting Sandy's treedome **for 30 seconds**, then cover it with a piece of paper and answer the questions below.

1 What **colour** is Sandy's bikini?
2 Was SpongeBob wearing **trousers**?
3 Does **Sandy** have an acorn, a cowboy or neither on her flag?
4 How many **jellyfish** could you see?
5 Something was missing. **What was it**?

Answers on page 88.

Jellyfish Fields Forever

SpongeBob and Patrick are hungry, so they've gone out to grab a treat. No, not Krabby Patties!

It's Jellyfish Jelly to jam into Jellyfish Jelly Jam (now say that ten times, fast!).

SpongeBob and Patrick need jelly from 10 jellyfish for their jam, so find the path through the maze that allows them to catch exactly that many.

But just remember – they can't travel along the same path twice or they'll get stung by the angry jellyfish!

Rearrange the letters below to find out how SpongeBob and Patrick get the jelly after the jellyfish are caught:

ezequse emth revy tengly

_____ / _____ /

_____ / _____

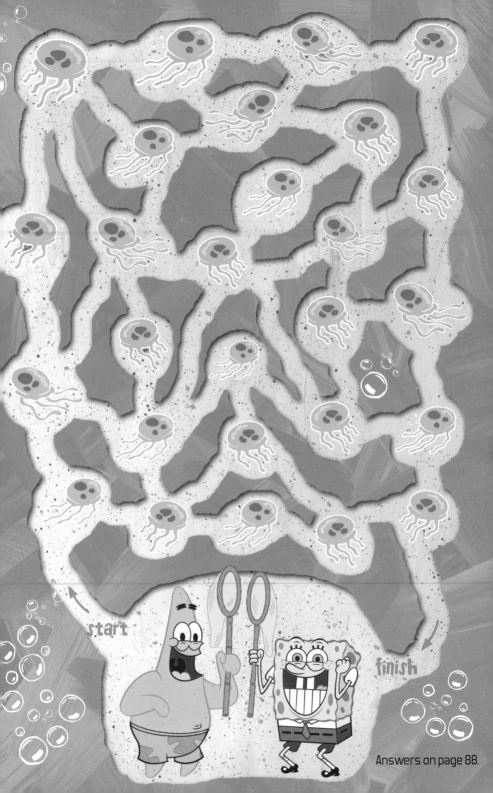

start

finish

Answers on page 88.

Bust a Move

A **rival dance crew** from New Kelp City is visiting Bikini Bottom and is **challenging SpongeBob** to a dance-off. SpongeBob really needs to find Patrick!

Which path leads to Patrick?

d

c

a b

SpongeBob and Patrick want a female dancer to join their duo. Can you guess who it is from the clues below?

1   It isn't Karen.
2   It isn't Pearl.
3   Her name rhymes with 'Candy Leeks'.

Answers on page 88.

Dancing with Squidward

Everyone says Squidward is **great** at dancing.
Or at least everyone whose name contains the words
'**Mr**', '**Squidward**' and '**Tentacles**' in that exact order.

Match the right shadow to Squidward '**entertaining**'
the Bikini Bottomites with his latest routine.

Which shadow is holding Squidward's
beloved clarinet? And which one is
holding his detested spatulas?

Answers on page 88.

Puzzled with Patrick ? ?

Patrick loves puzzles. Sometimes he even manages to compete one in a year! See if you can complete these in less time!

Join the Dots

Join the dots to find out what the **hidden picture** is.

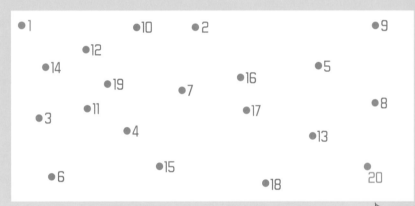

Food Jumble

Rearrange these letters to discover Patrick's favourite food.

c e r a m i c e ___ ___ ___ ___ / ___ ___ ___ ___ ___

I think my brain has frozen.

Answers on page 88.

Quick Draw

Here's how to draw Patrick:

1

Draw a rock

2

Draw Patrick
under the rock.

Try it below:

What kind of star
is Patrick?

The kind that's
not very bright.

What's Your Name?

What would you be called if you lived in Bikini Bottom?
Take this test to find out.

Instructions

1   Write your name on the **purple line** below.

2   Close your eyes and hold a pencil over the **blue words**
    on the opposite page. Then lower your pencil and write
    whichever word it lands on on the **blue line**.

3   Do this again with the **red** and orange words,
    writing the words on the same coloured line.

4   Your name is finished! Think it will catch on?

blue
. . . .

purple
. . . .

red
. . . .

orange
. . . .

bumpy	fuzzy	scratchy
loud	squishy	sloppy
happy	wet	super

fish	gherkin	nibble
seaweed	kipper	silly
flipper	cheese	patty

nose	bag	pants
hair	face	socks
trunks	bottom	fingers

Squishy Gary Cheese Bottom?

19

A Plague of Planktons

Yes, **Plankton** may be small – microscopic, even – but he's devious, sneaky and cunning.

SpongeBob panicked when he heard that Plankton was having himself cloned to make MULTIPLE Planktons. How would SpongeBob spot the REAL Plankton among the almost-perfect, hair-raising clones?

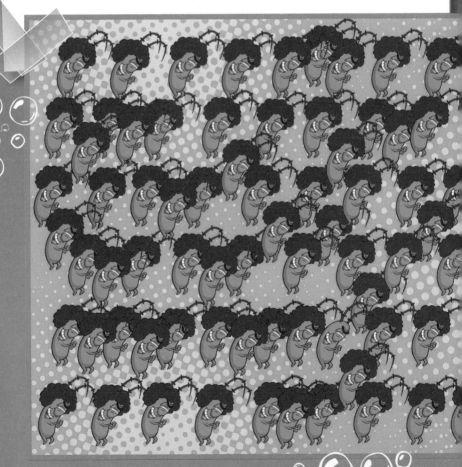

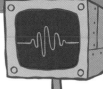

Plankton: 1% evil, 99% hot air.

This is where you come in.
Can **YOU** identify the real Plankton?

TRUE OR FALSE?
Plankton's first name is Sidney.

Answers on page 89.

Who Are You?

?
?

Which Bikini Bottomite are you most like?

Answer the **6 questions** below by ticking ✓ your answer, then add up your answers to find out **who you are!**

I You and your friend pose for a photo together. What do you do with the picture?

a ☐ Cut your friend out of the picture and then put the half with yourself in a frame.

b ☐ I'm not answering until I find out if this quiz costs anything!

c ☐ Put it in a frame by the side of your bed.

d ☐ What friend?

e ☐ Make a new flag for the top of your house. Awesome!

2 If you saw a penny on the street, what would you do?

a ☐ Ignore it. Bending down is too hard.

b ☐ Pocket it quickly and look for more.

c ☐ Oooooh! Shiny! Pick it up for my shiny penny collection.

d ☐ Oh, a penny! I can save it for my next try at world domination!

e ☐ I wouldn't notice it – I'm too busy having fun.

3 What do you think of Krabby Patties?

a ☐ Krabby Patties stole my dreams from me!

b ☐ They are a great way of making shiny, beautiful, irreplaceable money!

c ☐ I love them so much, I miss them when we are apart.

d ☐ I will get one some day!

e ☐ I'd rather be clam-wrestling.

4 What is your ambition?

a ☐ To be truly appreciated for the genius that I am.

b ☐ To own every dollar ever made.

c ☐ To be the best employee any employer ever had.

d ☐ World domination.

e ☐ To climb a mountain walking backwards, with my hands tied, wearing a blindfold.

Quiz continues on the next page!

5 What do you think of your house?

a ☐ I'd like it more if it weren't for my neighbour.

b ☐ It cost too much money. Houses should be free for rich people like me!

c ☐ It's the best place in the whole entire world, except where I work.

d ☐ I want it to be as big as the whole world.

e ☐ It would be better in Texas.

6 Life wouldn't be worth living without . . .

a ☐ Music and dance

b ☐ Money

c ☐ Friends

d ☐ Power

e ☐ Texas

Now **go back** through your answers and see **which letter** you ticked the most.

Mostly a — You're Squidward!

You're easily annoyed by everyone, especially your neighbours. But your self-belief is unshakeable!

Mostly b — You're Mr Krabs!

Money, money, money – that's what you live for. Though you do have a soft shell for your family.

Mostly c — You're SpongeBob!

Absorbent and yellow and porous are you! You're a whole heap of happy and are great fun to be around.

Mostly d — You're Plankton!

You're driven and determined, though only where world domination is concerned. If you turned your energy to something a little more positive, you'd have great potential.

Mostly e — You're Sandy Cheeks!

Energetic and bubbly, you're proud of your roots but always open to new experiences.

I Heart Dancing

One day in the Krusty Krab, SpongeBob just couldn't stop dancing. He danced around the kitchen. He danced around the till. He even danced around the tables while he was serving.

"You have to have **music** to dance," Squidward told him.

"I do have **music**. In my **mind**," said SpongeBob. "Oooh, I **LOVE** this one!"

And with that he carried on dancing, while Squidward watched him, seriously unimpressed.

"That is the **STUPIDEST** dance I've ever seen," he said to himself.

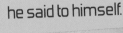

Later that day, SpongeBob was still dancing like a sponge with ants in his square pants. He danced right up to a table where a customer was waiting for her order.

"Your **Krabby Patty**, madam," SpongeBob said, handing her a plate.

"Thanks," she said. "By the way, I'm a **dance agent**. I have a **big star** who needs a great back-up dancer like you. Come to **my studio** tomorrow at noon and we'll do an **audition**."

SpongeBob almost exploded like a balloon of happiness. He was going to be in showbiz!

Squidward couldn't believe what he'd heard.
"**SpongeBob** got a dance audition?" he said
to himself. "That amoeba couldn't dance his way out of a
Krabby Patty wrapper!"

Squidward knew that he should be auditioning, not
SpongeBob. After all, he was the one with all the talent!
An idea popped into his jelly-like brain.
"To pass the audition, he'll have to **Practise** until he
drops," he whispered. "And when he does, I'll be there
ready to **take his place!**"

"Oh, SpongeBob," Squidward said in his nicest voice. "Why don't **I help you** with your audition? I could show you a few moves."

"Do you mean it, **Squidward?**" said SpongeBob. It was the kindest thing his neighbour had ever offered to do for him!

"Yes, but you must do **exactly** what I say," Squidward told him.

"I'll be **dance Putty** in yer hands!" SpongeBob beamed.

First, Squidward made SpongeBob run all the way to the top of Oyster Peak and back to get rid of his **flabby ankles**.

But before Squidward had even turned around to laugh at the genius of his plan, SpongeBob **was back** – and barely out of breath!

So Squidward taught SpongeBob how to *ribbon dance*. Everyone in Bikini Bottom knew that the ribbon dance was the hardest, most difficult, *imPossiblest* dance ever danced. SpongeBob would never be able to master it!

But SpongeBob was a **natural**. Soon his ribbon mermaids, dinosaurs and helicopters were twirling around in the ocean with him.

Squidward was the **angriest** he'd ever been – and he'd been quite angry in his time. The audition was getting **closer and closer** by the minute!

So Squidward decided he had to teach SpongeBob his own personal show-stopping move. It was a move so secret it can't even be written down, but SpongeBob was amazed.

"Are you **sure** I can do it?" SpongeBob wondered.

"You want to ace the **audition**, right?" Squidward asked. SpongeBob nodded. "So you're going to **practise** until you do it exactly like I just did! I don't care how long it takes."

What Squidward hadn't told SpongeBob was that you **needed tentacles** to get the move right, so he'd never be able to do it, no matter how much he **trained**. SpongeBob practised **all afternoon** ...

... and **all evening** ...

... and **all night** ... until **morning**, by which time SpongeBob was sleeping like a baby. Squidward **sniggered** to himself – his plan had worked perfectly! He slipped on his **leotard** and headed off to the audition.

At the studio, the agents were disappointed that SpongeBob hadn't shown up. But Squidward's dancing blew them all away, and soon they were begging him to be in the show.

"I knew it! **I AM** the greatest dancer," Squidward cheered. "What will I be **starring** in?"

"The **biggest show** Bikini Bottom has ever seen," the agents told him. "A new show starring ... **Squilliam!**"

"Sq...Sq...Sq...**what?**" spluttered Squidward. Ever since high school everything Squilliam touched had turned to gold, whereas everything Squidward touched turned to chum. Before Squidward knew it Squilliam had sauntered on stage and was now bossing him around!

"**Dance!**" Squilliam told him as he showed Squidward the new routine. "You're going to **Practise** until you do it exactly like I just did! I don't care how long it takes."

"Barnacles!" groaned Squidward. "**Wake uP**, SpongeBob, all is forgiven!"

The End

Puzzled with Patrick

Here's some stuff to help Patrick with. Tricky stuff. Fiddly stuff. Stuff so stuffy you could stuff your socks with it.

Muddle Up

Can you figure out which one of Patrick's friends' names is shown here?

dancey sheks

___ ___ ___ ___ ___ / ___ ___ ___ ___ ___

Odd One Out

Which picture of Mr Krabs and his moneybag is the odd one out?

a

b

c

Answers on page 89.

Take Away

You have 10 Krabby Patties and give SpongeBob and Squidward 5 each. SpongeBob manages to sell 1 more than Squidward, who has 1 left at the end of the day. How many did SpongeBob and Squidward each sell?

What Am I?

What is this riddle talking about?

What has a mouth but cannot eat?

Find a Way

Help SpongeBob find a way to Gary through this maze.

I can't understand anything ....

How to Draw SpongeBob

Ah, **SpongeBob**. So **handsome**. So dignified. So . . . **porous**. It's no wonder artists flock to his pineapple door, begging to paint him. But SpongeBob likes being yellow, so the artists just have to draw a picture instead.

Pablo Picatfish

Fincent Van Gogh

Eelnardo Da Vinci

Shellvador Dali

Turn to page 45, where you'll find a **bee-yootiful frame** in which to draw SpongeBob as you follow the instructions on the next few pages.

1

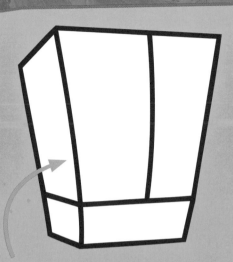

Use pencil so you can rub lines out later!

Start with a slightly wedge-shaped trapezium divided into sections .

2

For SpongeBob's cheek, draw a **semi circle** next to his right eye.

Next draw two **circles** resting on the centre line. The left circle should slightly overlap the right circle.

Draw his **mouth** and upper lip just below the eyes.

41

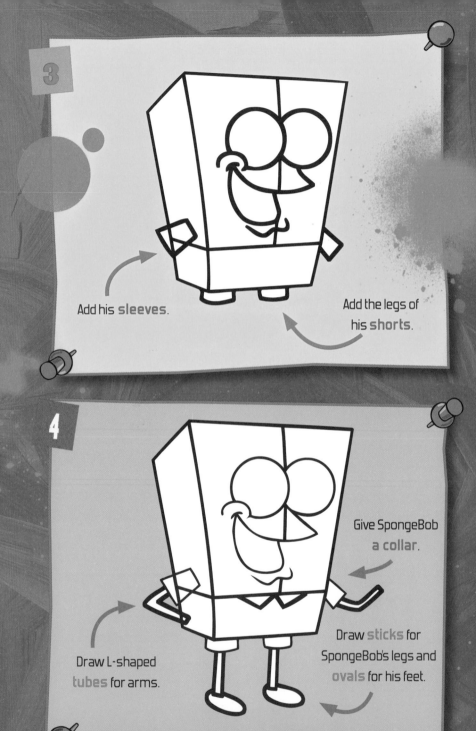

3

Add his **sleeves**.

Add the legs of his **shorts**.

4

Give SpongeBob a **collar**.

Draw **sticks** for SpongeBob's legs and **ovals** for his feet.

Draw L-shaped **tubes** for arms.

42

5

Add pupils to his **eyes**.

Draw a **nose** just below where his eyes meet. It should look like a **sideways finger**.

Draw his **tongue** inside his mouth.

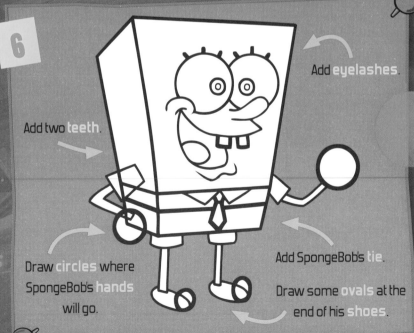

6

Add **eyelashes**.

Add two **teeth**.

Draw **circles** where SpongeBob's **hands** will go.

Add SpongeBob's **tie**.

Draw some **ovals** at the end of his **shoes**.

7

Erase the wedged **trapezium** that outlines his head and replace it with a **wavy** outline.

Add **fingers** and erase the original hand circles.

Add detail inside the **sleeve** and draw SpongeBob's **belt**.

Draw around both shapes for the **shoe** and erase the original ovals.

8

Draw in SpongeBob's spongy bits.

Draw in SpongeBob's **freckles** on his cheek.

Add some **socks** and shiny bits to his **shoes**.

When you've completed your picture of SpongeBob,
write your name below it.

by ....

What's the best paint to
paint SpongeBob with?

Watercolours!

The Sacred Recipe

Sheldon Plankton will stop at nothing to ruin Mr Krabs. He desperately wants his top-secret Krabby Patty recipe. He's even hidden inside a patty bun to get closer to snatching it, but he never succeeds.

But what's this? **Billowing Barnacles!** It seems as though Mr Krabs has taken pity on Plankton and given him the recipe! Read the instructions below to find out how you can decode it and make all Plankton's evil dreams come true!

Instructions

Delete all of these letters from the grid opposite to spell out Mr Krabs' famous krabby patty recipe!

b x 5, d x 4, f x 5, j x 3, m x 5, q x 3, s x 5, w x 4, k x 5, z x 3.

TRUE OR FALSE?
Mr Krabs and Plankton used to be best friends.

Why will Mr Krabs never share his recipe? Because he's **shellfish!**

g	b	d	o	f	j
m	q	t	s	w	k
s	c	m	f	k	h
b	j	a	d	s	m
z	f	k	z	i	b
l	m	w	l	q	w
f	n	s	d	z	e
k	b	v	w	e	f
r	q	k	t	s	j
m	e	d	l	b	l

__ __ __ __ __ __ / __ __ ' __ __ __ /

__ __ __ __ __ / __ __ __ __

Answer on page 89.

Ghostly Goings-on

What's that **ghostly shape** on the horizon, mateys? Help **SpongeBob** and **Patrick** work out which Bikini Bottomite is approaching!

Is it?

d
Mr Krabs

c
Sandy Cheeks

a
The Flying Dutchman

b
Plankton

What is the Flying Dutchman?

a) a piece of post
b) a pirate ghost
c) a slice of toast

It was the **Flying Dutchman**! He's come to gloat to SpongeBob and Patrick about his victory at the **Fancy Knotting** contest.

Add his **lowest** winning number of knots to his **highest** number of knots to reveal his **winning total** for this year.

3 Knots Knotted

5 Knots Knotted

6 Knots Knotted

4 Knots Knotted

3 Knots Knotted

Knots Knotted

Say this tongue twister ten times, fast. Don't let your tongue get tied up in knots!

Knotting neat knots needs knowledge

Ditchin'

SpongeBob and Patrick were excited beyond mere excitement. In fact, if their excitement were a fish, their excitement would be a fish that's as big as an aeroplane and as colourful as a rainbow that belches ticker-tape if you poked it.

THAT's how excited they were, because Mermaidman and Barnacleboy had written a book. Not only that, but they were doing a book signing in Bikini Bottom.

But there was one problem. "I **can't** go!" groaned SpongeBob. "I have to go to Boating School!"

"Can't you just **skip it**?" Patrick asked.

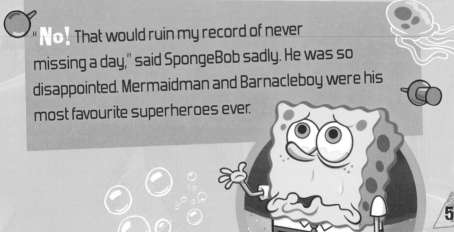

"**No!** That would ruin my record of never missing a day," said SpongeBob sadly. He was so disappointed. Mermaidman and Barnacleboy were his most favourite superheroes ever.

51

Patrick had another idea. "You could pretend you needed a long toilet break, then sneak out, get your book signed and sneak back in?" he said.

"But that's lying, Patrick, and lying is wrong," said SpongeBob. "I know! If I don't go to the toilet before tomorrow, then I'll really need to go, and it's not lying!"

And with that, their brilliant plan was complete.

By the next day, SpongeBob was the most
desperate he had ever been for the toilet.

"Don't dilly dally," said Mrs Puff as she gave him the
key for the toilets. "And make sure you bring that key
back!"

SpongeBob sprinted as fast as his thin legs would carry
him, and before long he'd finished in the toilets and leapt out
of the window, still holding Mrs Puff's key. Patrick was
waiting to meet him.

The friends made it to the book signing in record time. As they reached the front of the queue, their nerves set in. After all, Mermaidman and Barnacleboy were their heroes!

"Will you *sign our books* for us?" they babbled when they got to the front. Mermaidman and Barnacleboy signed their books for them happily.

"OK, that was **fun**," SpongeBob smiled as they left the signing. "Now I should **get back** to my class."

Patrick wasn't listening. He was gazing over his head, staring at a buzzing jellyfish.

"Ooh, SpongeBob, let's catch it," he said.

"What about my **class**?" SpongeBob said. "And we don't have any **nets**!"

It was too late. Patrick had already begun to run after the jellyfish, and before SpongeBob knew it, he was chasing after his friend.

When SpongeBob caught up with Patrick,
he found him eating ice cream.

"Patrick," said SpongeBob. "Where did the
jellyfish go?"

"What jellyfish?" said Patrick.

"I **have** to get back for my
class!" SpongeBob said. But
just then, he heard words
that made his eyes light up.

"You're my **hundredth** customer!" said the
ice-cream seller. "You boys can have all the
free ice cream you want!"
So SpongeBob and Patrick
tried every flavour in the
ice-cream cart. Twice.

After eating ice cream until his square pants began to feel tight, SpongeBob knew he should head back to class. He said farewell to Patrick and set his course for Mrs Puff's boating school.

But before he'd walked two spongy steps, he heard a familiar voice. "Where do you think you're goin', SquarePants?" It was Sandy Cheeks.

"I gotta get back to class," said SpongeBob. "I gave Mrs Puff my word!"

"C'mon, you've got time for a quick game of badminton with me and Dale," Sandy replied, twirling her badminton racquet.

"OK!" said SpongeBob. After all, he LOVED badminton.

SpongeBob got ready to serve. He adopted his special badminton pose, threw the shuttlecock in the air and raised his racquet to strike. But his arm wouldn't move! Someone was holding onto it.

"Not so fast, **yellow**," a police officer said. "You're playing with a wanted criminal."

"Sandy?" SpongeBob asked. He couldn't believe it!

"No. Dale," the officer told him as two other officers cuffed Dale. "He used to be such a good kid until he started **ditchin' class**. Now look at him."

SpongeBob screamed! Dale, a criminal? All because he'd ditched classes? He had to get back to Mrs Puff, or else one day he might end up in jail too.

SpongeBob ran and ran and ran and ran. He was so busy running that he didn't look where he was going, and he ran straight into the Bikini Bottom Hug Fest.

Bikini Bottom
HUG FEST

Fish were hugging him from every direction, making it impossible for him to carry on to Mrs Puff. And if he didn't get back soon, he was going to turn into a criminal! SpongeBob fought his way through the crowds . . .

... only to fall into the tar pits! SpongeBob began to sink into the sticky tar.

"I guess this is the **end** of SquarePants," he said as a single tear rolled down his cheek.

Just then, SpongeBob realised something. It wasn't the meaning of life. It wasn't the secret of happiness. It wasn't even where he'd hidden his Christmas presents so well that he couldn't find them again.

No – it was that he still had Mrs Puff's precious toilet key! He gathered all his strength and thrashed his way out of the tar like a sponge thrashing its way out of something very sticky. Soon he was free!

SpongeBob burst back into the classroom.

"I'm sorry, Mrs Puff!" he said. "Please **forgive me!**"

"I don't know what you mean, SpongeBob," replied Mrs Puff. "Anyway, I've got other problems. I'm in trouble for ditchin' **Jury Service**."

SpongeBob looked at her, amazed. He couldn't imagine Mrs Puff ditching anything!

"Let this be a lesson to you, SpongeBob," she continued. "**NEVER DITCH!**"

"OK Mrs Puff, I'll never ditch anything again," said SpongeBob as he packed up his belongings and left the classroom.

"**Good boy**, SpongeBob," said Mrs Puff before doing a double-take of what she'd just heard. "Hang on ... what do you mean **AGAIN?**"

The End

Excuses, Excuses

This isn't the first time SpongeBob has been late for Mrs Puff. Here are his five best excuses ever:

1 My bubble car popped.

2 I had to walk the snail.

3 A shark ate my car keys.

4 I'm rehearsing for my one-Sponge show about being late, and I'm staying in character.

5 I'm actually early for class – tomorrow!

Mrs Puff's patience is wearing thin though! Help SpongeBob come up with a new excuse to explain why he's late AGAIN.

SpongeBob was late because

. . . .

. . . .

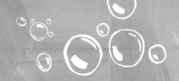

Booty-full

Find the two pictures of SpongeBob and Patrick out treasure hunting that are exactly the same. When you've found them, shout "yo ho ho and a bottle o' bubbles!"

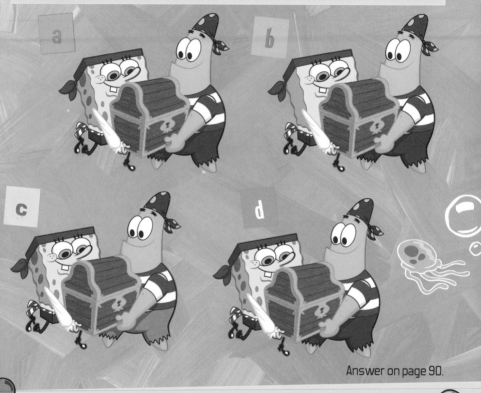

a

b

c

d

Answer on page 90.

What do you think might be in the treasure chest? Rubbish? Gold? Plankton's conscience? Draw it here.

Turnin' Up the Vibe

To make more money, **Mr Krabs** is holding a street dance contest at the Krusty Krab. **SpinMaster Sponge** is laying on the tunes, while **Body Poppin' Patrick** throws some star shapes on the floor.

These two pictures look the same, but there are
6 differences in picture 2. Find them all, then do your
best impression of SpongeBreak DancePants keepin' it real!

SpongeDoku

Use your **stickers** to complete this grid.

Place **a sticker** in each of the **empty boxes** so that each line, column and four-square box only contains one picture of each Bikini Bottomite..

Answer on page 90.

I Scream for Ice Cream

SpongeBob and Patrick both **LOVE** ice cream. SpongeBob's going to try a new Krabby Patty flavour. Bee-you-ti-ful!

Patrick's **favourite** flavour is ... whatever SpongeBob's is.

What's your favourite flavour of ice cream?

Create a new ice cream flavour that Mr Krabs can sell at the Krusty Krab using this plain cone. It can be whatever you like! Write your new ice cream's name below. Make sure Plankton's not in earshot though – he'll try to steal it!

SpongeBob SpeedyPants

SpongeBob can **flip more Krabby Patties** in a minute than anyone else could in an hour, a day or even **a lifetime**.

But in his hurry, he's got confused and made some of the Krabby Patties inside out, so the bun is in the middle! Find the ones he's made wrong before Mr Krabs docks his wages to make up for his mistake.

Oh no! Some **green ick** has got in one of the **burgers** – find that one too before it gets served up and the ick **spreads!**

Answers on page 90.

Gary, Gary, Wherefore Art Thou Gary?

Gary is SpongeBob's faithful **pet snail**, but he's got **lost** on a trip to the snail petting zoo!

Can you find Gary among all these **other snails**? He has **5 purple dots** on his **pink shell** and a **red swirl**.

When you find him, say '**Miaow**'.

Answer on page 91.

Funfair Ahoy!

Mr Krabs has made SpongeBob take a day off work, so to keep him from thinking about all the beautiful, **juicy Krabby Patties** he could be flipping, he's gone to the fairground with Patrick.

Can you find?

mayor

mail fish

old fish

police fish

Plankton has gone to the fairground to spy on SpongeBob. Try to find him in the scene – you may need a microscope!

Find the four fishy folk in the big scene and circle them. When you've found them all, see if you can find the objects too! The answers are on page 91.

Can you find?

candyfloss

teddy bear

balloons

hot dog

Sandcastles in the Sand

Today was a big day for SpongeBob and Patrick. It was their big shindig day, and they had planned to go to the beach together to celebrate their best-friendliness.

"I'm going to the beach with my best friend!" shouted SpongeBob.
"I'm going to the beach with my best friend!" shouted Patrick.
"I'm going to the beach with my best friend!" shouted SpongeBob.
"I'm going to the beach with my best friend!" shouted Patrick.
"I'm going to the beach with my best friend!" shouted SpongeBob.
"I'm going to the beach with my best friend!" shouted Patrick.
"I'm going to the beach with my best friend!" shouted SpongeBob.
"I'm going to the beach with my best friend!" shouted Patrick.

"We know," said all the other passengers on the bus. "Could you please be **quiet**?"

"Or," said SpongeBob. "We could sing you our song. From the top, Patrick. One and a two and a three ... **Best Friends** ..."

SpongeBob and Patrick were thrown off the bus faster than you could say "**get off**". Try saying it yourself. Yeah, that's how fast they were thrown off. But they didn't care. They walked to the beach, happy that they would be spending the rest of the day together.

At the beach, SpongeBob pulled out a surprise for Patrick. It was a small plastic disc that you throw.

"Hmmmmm," said SpongeBob. "If only small plastic disc that you throw had a shorter, catchier name."

"I know!" Patrick replied. "How about small plastic disc that you **toss**?"

"Perfect!" beamed SpongeBob. "Ready to play small plastic disc that you toss?"

Patrick giggled. "**Sure thing**, best friend!"

So SpongeBob tossed the small plastic disc as far as his arms would toss, and Patrick ran after it. He was so busy watching the small plastic disc that he didn't watch where he was going, and he ran straight into the lifeguard tower, knocking it over!

"You've destroyed the tower," shouted the lifeguard at poor Patrick, who was still clutching the small plastic disc that he'd caught.

"I'm sorry," he replied. "I was just playing with my best friend in the entire world over there!"

SpongeBob waved.

"Why don't you go play in the sand instead," said the lifeguard angrily. "I'm sure your stupidity can't ruin anything there."

Patrick was upset. After all, everyone in Bikini Bottom knew his stupidity could destroy anything it wanted.

"Playing with sand sounds pretty **boring**," said Patrick.

"Ah, come on buddy," smiled SpongeBob. "We can build sandcastles. It'll be as **scrumptiously** happy as a barrel of candy canes on a unicorn."

Patrick nodded. After all, that did sound scrumptiously happy.

So the two best friends picked up their buckets and spades and started sandcastle-ing.

Soon, SpongeBob and Patrick had begun to make their sandcastles. SpongeBob's had three turrets and a moat, while Patrick's had only one turret and a drawbridge.

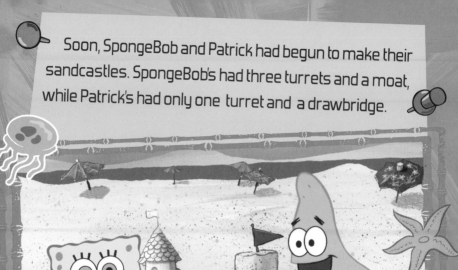

SpongeBob glanced up at Patrick's sandcastle. "How's it going?" he asked.

"Everything's just **fine and dandy** in Patrick's kingdom," came the reply as Patrick struggled with another turret.

"Here buddy, let me help you out," SpongeBob offered. But as he reached for his bucket and spade, SpongeBob accidentally put his elbow into the corner of Patrick's castle! Patrick was furious.

"You destroyed my castle!"
Patrick roared.

"I was only trying to **help!**"
said SpongeBob, defending himself.

"Well perhaps I could **help you** too, 'best friend',"
Patrick replied, and before SpongeBob could stop him,
Patrick thumped his hand straight through his castle!
Now both of them had to start from scratch.

They rebuilt their castles in silence. It was so quiet you could hear the tiny cogs ticking in Patrick's mind.

"Erm, Patrick," said SpongeBob.

"What?" Patrick replied moodily.

"You built on my side," SpongeBob told him.

"So?"

"So," said SpongeBob through gritted teeth. "It isn't allowed – that's my side." And with that, he smashed down Patrick's wall.

"There," said SpongeBob. "That's better!"

"You **tyrant!**" Patrick screamed. "You'll pay for that!" The drawbridge of Patrick's castle lowered and hundreds of sand warriors marched out. They had sand cannons, sand armour and even sand horses.

"You call **THAT** an army?" mocked SpongeBob. "Whatever."

The front doors of SpongeBob's castle opened to reveal an even bigger army of sand robots, complete with sand lasers, sand spaceships and sand tanks.

"Prepare for **war!**" shouted SpongeBob. "**CHAAAAAAAAAAAAAARGE!**"

And so began the First Great Sand War!

KABOOM! SpongeBob's sand robots blew up Patrick's drawbridge.

KAPOW! Patrick's sand warriors destroyed SpongeBob's turrets.

KAPATTY! The two brave generals sat together and ate Krabby Patties as the battle unfolded, before quickly remembering that they were now mortal enemies and running back to take charge of their forces.

After what felt like hours, the sand forces of SpongeBob the Great and Patrick the Mighty began to dwindle into small heaps of sand. They desperately tried to carry on fighting, but their strength slowly ebbed away.

SpongeBob and Patrick looked at each other, and at the huge sandy mess around them.

"What happened?" asked Patrick sadly.

"I got **carried away**," said SpongeBob. He was upset that he'd wasted his special day with his best friend fighting with him through the medium of sand. "I'm sorry, Patrick."

"I got carried away as well, SpongeBob," sighed Patrick. "**I'm sorry**, too."

"Best friends again?" SpongeBob smiled.

"Best friends again," Patrick beamed back at his spongy buddy before they gave each other a big hug.

"Let's get this mess cleaned up before that cranky lifeguard sees it," said SpongeBob.

"I bet I can clean it up **quicker**," said Patrick.

"No, **I** can," said SpongeBob.

"No you can't."

"Yes I can."

"No you can't."

"Yes I can."

"No you can't."

"Yes I can ..."

The End

Star Pupil

Give your brain cells a workout and answer these tricky questions. There's a **very special prize** up for grabs!

1

What is SpongeBob's dream?

a To run the Chum Bucket
b To pass his Boat Driving test
c To leave Bikini Bottom

2

What noise does Gary make?

a Woof
b Baa
c Miaow

3

Where does Patrick live?

a Under a rock
b At the Krusty Krab
c With Squidward

4

What kind of animal is Pearl?

a A squirrel
b A whale
c A starfish

5

Sandy Cheeks comes from Schmexas. **True or False?**

a True
b False

6

What instrument does Squidward play (badly)?

a The saxophone
b The piano
c The clarinet

7

What do Mr Krabs and Pearl live in?

a An anchor

b A boat

c The cash register at the Krusty Krab

8

Who has been to college?

a Karen

b Plankton

c Patrick

9

What do SpongeBob and Sandy like to do together?

a Plait their hair

b Sit and stare into space

c Practise karate

Now check your answers on page 91!

Results

How many questions did you **get right?**
Write **your name** in the space below and **your score**
in the porthole, then **claim your prize!**

. . . .

Points Mean Prizes!

6-9 Dinner at Krusty Krab

3-5 No dinner at all

0-2 Dinner at the Chum Bucket

Answers

Page 10 SpongeBob SillyFaces

False – SpongeBob is made of sponge. The clue is in his name.

Page 11 Memory Test

1 **Purple**, like always.
2 **Yes** – made you look though.
3 **An acorn**. She's a squirrel after all.
4 **None**. If you saw any, you need to get your eyes tested. .
5 **Ice cream!** Everyone knows no picture is complete without ice cream.

Page 12-13 Jellyfish Fields Forever

See solution (right)
How do SpongeBob
and Patrick get the jelly?
Squeeze them very gently

Page 14 Bust a Move

Path **d** leads to Patrick.
SpongeBob and Patrick want
Sandy Cheeks to join their crew.

Page 15 Dancing with Squidward

Picture **4** is the matching shadow.
Shadow **1** is holding Squidward's clarinet
Shadow **3** is holding his spatulas.

Page 16 Puzzled with Patrick

Join the Dots – It's the trail Gary left over Patrick's back yard.
Food Jumble – Patrick's favourite food is **ice cream**.
After all, everyone knows cera mice are poisonous!

Page 20-21 A Plague of Planktons

The real Plankton is circled in red. **True or False** – False. Plankton's first name is Sheldon, which his wife Karen thinks is hilarious.

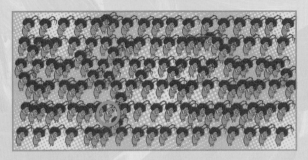

Page 38-39 Puzzled with Patrick

Muddle Up – The hidden name was **Sandy Cheeks**.

Odd One Out – Picture **b** is the odd one out because the moneybag had 10 more dollars inside.

Take Away – SpongeBob sold **5** Krabby Patties. Squidward sold **4** Krabby Patties.

What Am I – **A river**. Or anyone who's ever been to the Chum Bucket

Find a Way –

Page 46-47 The Sacred Recipe

The secret message reads **'Gotcha I'll never tell'**.

True – then they fell out over the Krabby Patty recipe!

Page 48-49 Ghostly Goings-on

The shadow matches picture **a** – the Flying Dutchman.

The Flying Dutchman is **b)** a pirate ghost.

He knotted **3+6=9** knots to win this year.

Page 63 Booty-full

Pictures **a** and **d** are the same.

Page 64–65 Turnin' Up the Vibe

Page 66 SpongeDoku

Page 68 SpongeBob SpeedyPants

The inside out Krabby Patties are circled in red.

The burger with ick is circled in blue.

Page 69 Gary, Gary, Wherefore Art Thou Gary?

Page 70-71 Funfair Ahoy!

Plankton is circled in green.

Page 84-86 Star Pupil

1. b – to pass his Boat Driving test; **2. c** – miaow; **3. a** – under a rock;
4. b – a whale; **5. b** – false; **6. c** – the clarinet; **7. a** – an anchor;
8. b – Plankton; **9. c** – practise karate.

E0826